SNAKE ATTACK!

Adapted by Tracey West

D1052124

SCHOLASTIC INC.

ISBN 978-0-545-46518-2

12 11 10 9 8 7 6 5 4 3 2 1   12 13 14 15 16 17/0

Printed in the U.S.A.   40
First printing, September 2012

CONTENTS

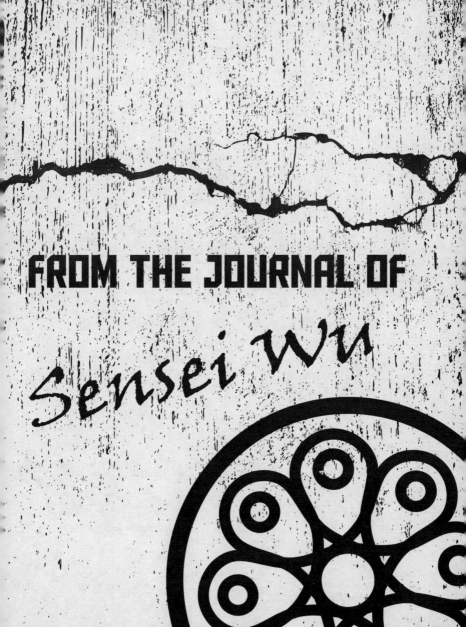

FROM THE JOURNAL OF

Sensei Wu

hat is the best way to defeat an enemy?

I challenged my four ninja with this riddle, and none of them could determine the correct answer. They suggested training, teamwork, and planning, which are all necessary, but they are not the best answer to the question. To find that answer, my ninja needed to look deeper inside themselves.

For quite some time, they were focused on trying to defeat one enemy: my nephew, Lloyd Garmadon. Lloyd is just a boy, but his

fate was set the day he was born. His father is the evil Lord Garmadon, my brother.

Young Lloyd does not have the evil heart that his father does, yet he has managed to cause a great deal of trouble. After Lord Garmadon was banished from Ninjago, Lloyd tried to follow in his footsteps. He unleashed two of the ancient Serpentine tribes.

The part-serpent, part-human Serpentine are cold-blooded and ruthless. Lloyd thought he had enough power to control them, but once the snake warriors had used him for their own gain, they cast him aside. Lloyd's efforts were not a failure, as he retrieved something very valuable — the Map of Dens. The Map of Dens is a rare scroll that holds the secret locations of all five Serpentine tribes.

Seeking revenge on the two tribes that had wronged him — the Hypnobrai and the Fangpyres — Lloyd followed the map to the

tomb of a third tribe, the Anacondrai. There, he found Pythor, the Anacondrai general. The large, purple serpent was surrounded by the skeletons of his fallen comrades. The last of the Anacondrai, he is as charming as he is treacherous. Pythor offered to befriend my lonely nephew, and Lloyd eagerly accepted.

Sadly, Lloyd had not yet learned that snakes should not be trusted. They set a trap for the ninja at the Boarding School for Bad Boys. When the trap failed, Pythor stole the Map of Dens from Lloyd, and left him to be captured by the ninja.

Cole, Zane, Kai, and Jay all suggested suitable punishments for Lloyd. However, I had another plan. I brought my nephew back to our ship, *Destiny's Bounty*, tucked him into bed, and read him a story.

For the first time, I saw a peaceful look of contentment on Lloyd's face.

"I'm sorry, Uncle," he told me, but he did not need to apologize.

My ninja did not understand, and they became angry.

"Why isn't the little brat getting punished?" Jay asked me.

"It's not fair," Cole complained.

You see, they had not yet learned the answer to the riddle: What is the best way to defeat an enemy? And the answer is, of course, to make that enemy your friend.

Lloyd lives with us now, and while he has much to learn, I have faith that he will follow the goodness that has always been in his heart. In the meantime, my ninja have found another distraction to consume them: the identity of the Green Ninja.

Their obsession began when they read one of my secret scrolls. The scroll predicts that a Green Ninja will rise who is powerful enough to defeat Lord Garmadon. Each ninja

secretly hopes that he will become the Green Ninja. They spend many precious minutes arguing about which one of them it is.

I fear that this distraction may be harmful in the long run. They must not lose focus. Now that Pythor has the Map of Dens, he will be able to awaken the remaining Serpentine tribes. And if the snake warriors join forces, it will become nearly impossible to stop them. Ninjago has never seen such a threat. I must trust that Cole, Zane, Kai, and Jay will rise to the challenge — and I will do my best to guide them through these dark times.

ENTER THE SAMURAI

High in the blue skies over Ninjago, *Destiny's Bounty* was perched on top of a tall mountain peak. The ship was an impressive vessel. Painted the color of red flame, its prow was shaped like a fierce dragon's head with yellow eyes and sharp yellow teeth. Its sails, white streaked with red, looked like a dragon's wings.

At the stern of the ship was a yellow house with a black roof. This is where the ninja lived and trained. The busiest room inside the ship was the mission control center, which was filled with control panels and computer

screens. On this sunny day, a large map of Ninjago was projected on the control room's wall. Nya, Kai's sister, pointed to the map.

"Last we heard of Pythor, he stole the Map of Dens from Lloyd and is now on his way to open the last two Serpentine tombs," Nya said.

"Don't remind me," Lloyd Garmadon said shamefully.

"Pythor is our most **dangerous threat**," Sensei Wu reminded them. "If he finds those tombs before we do, with his intellect and all of the tribes unleashed, there's no telling what he will do."

"But those tombs could be anywhere," Jay pointed out. "Without the Map of Dens, we might as well just throw darts at the map."

Nya grinned. "Good idea. Why don't we?"

She expertly threw two darts at once, and each landed in a different spot on the map. "These are the two locations of the Hypnobrai and Fangpyre tombs," she explained. Then

she walked to the map and put in one more dart. "And *this* is Pythor's tomb. After many hours studying the map, I discovered a secret pattern."

Nya shone a flashlight on the map, and a red pattern of the Ninjago symbol for *serpent* overlapped the map. By looking at the symbol, it was easy to see where in Ninjago the other tombs were located.

"There is little time," said Sensei Wu. "Kai and Jay, you head to the Venomari tomb. Cole and Zane, you take the Constrictai tomb."

Sensei Wu handed Cole a wooden flute with a red swirl pattern painted on it. The Sacred Flute had the power to stop the Serpentine. "Take this. You might need it if you run into Pythor. Good luck, ninja."

Nya sighed. "What am I going to do?" she wondered aloud.

"Nya, I need you here to make sure Lloyd doesn't get into any more trouble," Sensei replied.

"Yes, Sensei," Nya said sadly.

"We've got some snakes to club!" Cole cried.

"Let's get some!" said Jay, and with that the ninja sped off.

Each ninja transformed his Weapon of Spinjitzu into a supercharged vehicle. Cole's Scythe of Quakes became the Tread Assault, a rugged dune buggy with powerful wheels that could ride over the toughest terrain. Zane's Shurikens of Ice became the Ice Mobile, a sleek speed machine. Jay's Nunchucks of Lightning became the Storm Fighter, a fast fighter jet. And Kai's Sword of Fire transformed into the supersized Blade Cycle.

The ninja split up. Zane and Cole followed the map across the desert to a tall, narrow mountain. They climbed all the way to the top to reach the Constrictai tomb. When they arrived, they found a hole in the top of the mountain, and a rope leading down into the dark interior.

"Looks like Pythor was already here," Zane guessed. "Maybe we should check it out."

Zane quickly climbed down the rope and found himself in a dark cave. He lit up a flare and looked around. Strange drawings were carved into the cave walls.

"Didn't Momma Snake ever tell them not to draw on the wall?" Cole asked after he climbed down.

"Well, it says here that there is a legend that the snake tribes will unite," Zane said, reading the drawings. "Then they can find the four Silver Fang Blades that will **unleash the Great Devourer** . . . an evil that will consume all of the land, turning day into night."

"You got all that from those little pictures?" Cole remarked.

"This gives me deep concern. If Pythor reunites all the tribes before Kai and Jay can find him —"

"Relax, Zane, they're a bunch of dumb snakes that believe in fairy tales." He paused. Suddenly, the ground underneath them began to shake. "Wait, did you feel that? Don't move!"

Boom! A Constrictai warrior erupted from the floor of the cave. He had shiny black and orange scales, glowing yellow eyes, sharp fangs, and black spikes sticking out of his head. The warrior quickly wrapped his tail around Zane.

"I've been waiting for you," he hissed. "Pythor sends his regards."

Cole sprang into action. *"Ninjaaago!"* he yelled, plunging his Scythe of Quakes into the ground, shaking the entire cavern. The Constrictai let go of Zane and disappeared underground.

"Zane, go for the rope!" Cole yelled.

Zane ran — and then heard Cole scream behind him. He looked back to see his friend being pulled under the floor. Then Cole shot

back up and landed with a thud on his back.

But the Constrictai wasn't finished with him. He tunneled under the ground, heading right for Cole. Cole quickly pulled out the Sacred Flute and began to play. But before the song could take effect, the Constrictai wrapped his tail around Cole, squeezing him tightly. The flute fell from Cole's hands.

"Ninjaaago!" Zane yelled. He turned into a spinning tornado and retrieved the flute before the Constrictai could get it. He began to play, but the Constrictai reached out and grabbed him by the throat. Now the snake warrior had both ninja in his clutches!

But Zane didn't give up. He brought the flute to his lips and, breathing as hard as he could, began to play. The sound made the snake warrior roar in pain. He let go of his grip on Zane and Cole.

"Wrap your head around this!" Cole cried. He picked up his Scythe and whacked the Constrictai hard, knocking him out.

"Good one," Zane said.

"Thanks," Cole replied. "But if he was expecting us, I think Kai and Jay are also walking into a trap. Come on. Let's get out of here."

Meanwhile, Kai and Jay had followed the map to a dense, dark jungle that led to a green, slimy swamp. They exited their vehicles and walked until they reached the water. Jay sniffed the air and made a face at Kai. It smelled disgusting!

"It's not me," Kai protested. "We're in the Toxic Bogs. This stuff will eat through you worse than Cole's chili." He then took a nearby twig and dipped it in the water. When he pulled it out, the part that was in the water had been burned off.

Since swimming wasn't an option, the ninja swung on vines until they reached solid ground—and the entrance to a cave blocked by a stone with strange markings.

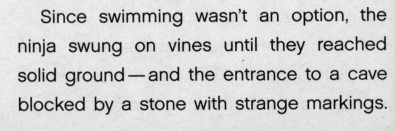

Jay pushed near the stone, and the door slid open to reveal a deep, dark cave.

"Pe-ew!" Jay complained, as an even worse stench filled the air. His voice echoed back to him. *Pe-ew!* Jay laughed.

While Jay looked around in the cave and had fun with the echo, Kai patrolled the outside of the cave.

"This place looks empty; we must've just missed Pythor," Jay said.

Then, Kai heard a rustling noise. He followed the sound until he found a purple swamp toad sitting on a log in the water.

"You shouldn't sneak up on me like that," Kai told the toad. "If I wasn't such a well-trained nin—"

An evil laugh interrupted him as the log slowly began to rise from the water. It wasn't a log at all—it was the flat green-and-black head of a Venomari!

The snake warrior spat nasty green venom in Kai's face. He cried out as the poison stung

his eyes. When he opened them, everything around him looked strange and blurry.

Dozens of Serpentine soldiers emerged from the swamp. Their heads looked like snakes, but they had human arms and legs. There were green-and-black Venomari and orange-and-black Constrictai. Kai knew this could only mean one thing—they were too late! Pythor had already reached both tombs and unleashed the Serpentines.

Then the Venomari poison started to make Kai see even stranger things. To him, the snake warriors looked like creepy gingerbread men and elves. He wildly swung his Sword.

"Oh, this is not good! Jay! Jay!" he cried.

Jay ran out of the cave to his friend's side. But the two ninja were quickly outnumbered by the Serpentine.

"There are so many elves and gingerbread people . . . everywhere!" Kai said.

"Okay, I don't know what you're seeing, but this is no time to lose yourself. I need you, partner!" Jay replied.

"I've never fought elves before. We're toast!" Kai screamed.

Then a roar came from the jungle, and the Tread Assault and the Ice Mobile plowed through the trees. Cole and Zane soared over the poisonous swamp. Their vehicles morphed back into weapons in midair, and Cole and Zane landed next to their friends.

"Anyone order a little kick butt?" Cole cried.

Butt! Butt! Butt! his voice echoed, and Jay laughed and looked back into the dark tomb.

"BOO!"

A terrifying Serpentine with gleaming purple scales, sharp white fangs, and glowing magenta eyes shot out of the cave. It was Pythor! With his long neck and even longer tail, he towered over the

21

other Serpentine — and the ninja.

Thinking quickly, Zane picked up the Sacred Flute and began to play. In a flash, Pythor's powerful tail lashed out, wrapped around the flute, and took it right out of Zane's hands.

"Let's not let music ruin things," Pythor hissed in a chilling voice.

The Serpentine marched toward the four ninja, forcing them to back up into the swamp. With nowhere else to go, they jumped and landed on a big green log floating in the swamp. But the log was slowly disappearing as the poisonous water burned through it.

"I've got a *sinking* feeling this may be the last I see of you four," Pythor said with an evil laugh.

The ninja were trapped. As the log drifted away, they were too far from shore to jump and battle the Serpentine. The vines overhead were too high to reach. The log sizzled in the toxic goo under their feet.

"That's it. I used to hate dragons, but now I officially hate snakes," Cole said, defeated.

Kai's eyes were still cloudy from the venom. "Wait. Do you see that? A magic floating rope!" he said as he reached toward an imaginary rope hanging in front of the log.

Jay caught Kai right before he fell off the log. "Wow, that Venomari venom is some powerful stuff," Jay said.

"For whatever it is worth, it was an honor to fight beside you all," Zane solemnly told his friends.

Suddenly, a rope dropped from the sky right in front of them!

"The magic rope . . ." Kai said in a daze.

"Quick! Everyone grab it and climb over!" Jay yelled.

As they reached for the rope, something even more amazing came down from the sky. A giant metal robot landed in front of the tomb, its **jet engines roaring**. The robot had a red metal

body that looked like a samurai warrior's costume, and a black samurai helmet on its head.

The Samurai raised his right hand, and a powerful net shot out at the Serpentine troops. They scattered as the net landed on two Constrictai warriors, who quickly tunneled underground. The Venomari jumped into the swamp to escape. Only Pythor was left.

"Oh, dear," he said, slinking backward.

A hydraulic squeal came from the robot as a cage on the Samurai's chest opened up to reveal an actual samurai warrior inside. He was dressed in red, with a black chest shield, a black helmet, and a red face guard covering his lower face. His eyes looked red and menacing.

"Pythor target confirmed," he said in a deep voice. "Time to bag . . . and tag."

As Pythor turned and hurried away, the Samurai shot a dart with a homing device

into his tail. Pythor vanished into the jungle, and the Samurai jumped down from the robot.

"Wh-who are you?" Cole asked.

"How about the coolest thing I've ever seen!" Jay cheered.

"Santa?" Kai asked, still affected by the Venomari poison.

Zane stepped forward and held out his hand. "Thank you, mysterious warrior. I owe you my life for saving —"

Pfffff! The Samurai held out his right hand and a cloud of gas swirled around Zane. He fell backward and began to snore.

"Hey! That wasn't nice!" Jay said.

But before the others could protest, the Samurai put them to sleep, too. Then he jumped back into his robot and rocketed away.

Fortunately for the ninja, Sensei Wu found them and brought them safely aboard the ship. When they woke up, they were

all confused. As they ate dinner, they told Sensei, Nya, and Lloyd what had happened.

"So then, just as we were going to bite it, this huge mechanical robot—" Jay was saying.

"Samurai. It was a samurai," Zane corrected him.

"A sama-what?" Lloyd asked.

"Samurai," repeated Sensei Wu. "The highest level of warrior class. They would protect nobility and serve with honor on the battlefield."

"He was a hundred feet high, with weapons coming out of every part of him." Kai paused, leaning in to Cole. "Look at Sensei's beard. It moves like snakes," he whispered.

"When is this Venomari spit supposed to wear off? It's starting to get annoying," Nya commented.

"Okay, don't let this mysterious samurai cloud what's really important," Cole reminded everyone. "Zane and I read about

it when we were at the Constrictai tomb. All the Serpentine are out, and if Pythor can unite them, the legend states that some Great Devourer is going to consume the land. . . ."

"Great Devourer?" Nya asked.

Lloyd moaned. "It's all my fault! If I hadn't opened the first hatch, none of this would have happened."

"We cannot change the past, but we can affect the future. At least we have the Sacred Flute in our possession," Sensei Wu said.

Jay shrugged sheepishly. "Yeah, about that . . ."

"Pythor sort of . . . stole it," Zane admitted.

A cloud crossed Sensei Wu's face. "The last Sacred Flute? Gone?"

He looked at the four ninja, his dark eyes blazing. "You four are Ninjago's last hope!"

CHAPTER 1

Destiny's Bounty flew across the sky, searching for any sign of Pythor and the Serpentine. Inside, the ninja, Nya, and Lloyd were taking a tea break around the low wood table in the dining room. Lloyd bragged about what he would do if he found a snake warrior.

"First, I'd stomp on his tail," Lloyd said, pounding the table with his fist. "Then, when he turns, a thunderclap to his ears. Then, when he's stunned, I'll disarm him!"

Cole laughed. "Too late. He's already hypnotized you and you're now under his

control," he said, thinking of the powers of the Hypnobrai tribe.

"Or he's already put you in a squeeze," Zane said, remembering the Constrictai.

"Or maybe he's bit you and you're slowly turning into a snake," Jay added, shuddering slightly. That's exactly what the Fangpyres had done to Jay's parents before the ninja saved them.

Kai's memories of the Venomari were still fresh. "Or spit on you with hallucinatory venom. Trust me, bad stuff."

Sensei Wu walked in carrying a package. He had a cheerful expression on his face.

"Uncle, what's the best way to stun a Serpentine if you don't know what kind it is?" Lloyd asked.

The sensei frowned. "Sadly, it was the Sacred Flute you four carelessly lost."

"Whoa, whoa, whoa, we didn't lose it. Pythor *stole* it," Jay said.

"Whatever the case, without it I fear we

have nothing to **combat their powers**. We may have prevented them from uniting in the past, but they will try again. And one day they will be stronger," Sensei explained.

"Don't worry, Sensei," Cole said confidently. "I've almost reached my full potential. When I become the Green Ninja, we're not gonna need a magical flute."

Kai shook his head. "*You're* gonna be the Green Ninja? Ha-ha-ha. Don't make me laugh."

"I thought it was decided that I was destined to become the Green Ninja," Zane said.

Jay laughed and put a hand on his friend's shoulder. "The only thing decided about you, Zane, is that you're weird!"

The four ninja began to argue noisily about which one of them would become the Green Ninja. Lloyd was more interested in Sensei Wu's package.

"What's in the box?" he asked.

Sensei Wu smiled and removed the lid. "Your new uniforms!"

The ninja stopped arguing and rushed over to the box. Each ninja had the same color uniform as before: black for Cole, red for Kai, blue for Jay, and white for Zane. But the fabric was lighter and stronger, and each one had cool new features, like protective armor and built-in weapons.

"Whoa, they've got, like, armor!" said Jay.

"I love the highlights," Kai added.

"Aww, nothing for me?" Lloyd asked.

"Umm, you get, uh"—Sensei hesitated—"the box," Sensei said, handing the box to a disappointed Lloyd.

Beep! Beep! Beep! Beep!

Before the ninja could try on their uniforms, the ship's high-pitched alarm rang out. They raced to the bridge, where Cole started enlarging an image on a computer monitor. It showed snake warriors chasing frightened citizens.

"Sorry to break up the moment, boys, but a small faction of our slithering friends are stirring up trouble over at Mega-Monster Amusement Park," Cole reported.

Lloyd began to jump up and down. "Amusement park? Can I go with you? *Please?* Let me make things up to you. I can help!"

"I'm sorry, nephew," Sensei Wu said kindly. "You will stay here, where it's safe."

Lloyd moaned. "Aw. Ninja get all the fun!"

Jay looked at his friends. "What do you say, guys? Time to try out the new merchandise?"

Moments later the ninja stood on the rails of the ship in their new uniforms. Each ninja held his golden weapon in his hand.

"This new material feels like it'll protect us more," Cole said, admiring his uniform.

"Yet provide more mobility," Zane added.

"You want to strut your stuff on the catwalk, or get down to that amusement park so we can go on some rides?" Jay asked impatiently.

"I love a good old-fashioned roller coaster, but nothing beats this!" Kai cried. With a whoop, he jumped off of the railing, and his friends followed.

The weapons quickly transformed into **Spinjitzu vehicles**. The Tread Assault, Ice Mobile, Storm Fighter, and Blade Cycle zoomed through the sky until they reached the amusement park. Then the vehicles morphed back into weapons as the ninja landed, feetfirst, on the ground.

A tall, hilly roller coaster wrapped around the circular amusement park. A Ferris wheel with brightly colored seats rose high into the sky. A red-and-yellow-striped post topped with a spinning disc with dangling swings towered above all of the other rides. The ninja walked among colorful game booths and snack stands toward a crowd of cheering girls.

"Ladies, relax, we have arrived!" Jay said with a wave.

But the girls didn't even notice the ninja.

Curious, the ninja made their way through the crowd. In the center, half a dozen Serpentine were tied up with thick rope.

"What just happened?" Kai asked one of the bystanders, a teenage girl with brown hair and glasses.

"Oh, you, like, totally missed it!" she swooned. "There were, like, icky snakes, and then this mysterious samurai came in and saved everyone."

Next to her, a blonde-haired girl had a dreamy look in her eyes. "He was, like, gorgeous!"

"You saw his face?" Kai asked.

"No, but we could totally tell," insisted the first girl.

Just then, Nya walked up and handed each girl a strawberry ice cream cone.

Jay was happy to see her. "Nya, you're here!"

"Yeah, you just missed all the action," she said. "He just flew in, took care of business,

and then flew off. It was pretty cool."

Then a young boy's angry voice got their attention.

"I don't want to be a ninja!" the little boy cried to his mom. He was wearing a blue ninja costume. "I want to be a samurai!"

The ninja looked at one another in frustration. They were used to being the good guys of Ninjago.

"Who *is* this guy?" Kai asked.

Cole looked angry. "Whoever he is, he's **stealing our thunder**

CHAPTER 2

'm gonna say it. I hate samurai!" Jay folded his arms across his chest.

Sensei Wu wandered over, holding a fluffy pink cloud of cotton candy. "Do I hear a hint of jealousy? Maybe this can be a lesson for you," he said.

Jay sighed. "Not another lesson!" he complained. "Hey, wait, how did you get here so quickly?"

"The lesson is . . . 'iron sharpens iron,'" Sensei Wu replied, ignoring his question.

Zane shook his head. "I do not follow, Sensei."

"Healthy competition can help you reach your true potential faster," he told them. "Do not be jealous of this samurai. Let it inspire."

Then his eyes lit up. "Ooh, Ferris wheel!" he cheered, running off.

"Inspire?" Jay's voice was doubtful.

"Wait a minute," Kai said. "Maybe the old man's right."

"Compete with the Samurai?" Cole asked in disbelief. "He's got all the cool gadgets. We don't stand a chance!"

"No, not with him, with us," Kai explained. "I say we turn this into our own competition. We all want to know which one of us is best."

"You mean, which of us is the Green Ninja," Jay corrected him.

"Yeah, well, whoever is skilled enough to catch this mysterious samurai is probably the best of the bunch," Kai pointed out.

Jay finally got it. "So whoever learns the identity of this samurai is the one who will become the destined Green Ninja. I love it!"

"Then it's a bet," Cole said.

"May the Green Ninja win," said Kai.

The ninja raised their weapons in the air.

"Ninjaaaaago!"

They did not have to wait long to begin their competition. Now that they were free, bands of Serpentine were roaming Ninjago, causing trouble everywhere. The Samurai was sure to turn up soon.

Zane answered a call for help in the Glacier Barrens in the frozen north. A gang of Hypnobrai were terrorizing the igloo-dwelling inhabitants of a small village. Zane used his Ice Mobile to speed up and down the icy hills as subzero winds whipped past him.

But when he reached the village, he found the Hypnobrai tied up—right next to the Samurai, who rocketed away before Zane could get a glimpse of his face.

"Metal menace!" Zane yelled, hurling a snowball into the sky.

Kai came to the rescue of three young maidens in the Wildwood Forest. He raised his Sword of Fire and charged at three orange-and-black Constrictai.

"Go, ninja, go!" the maidens cheered.

But before he could even fight the Serpentine, a net swooped out of nowhere and captured the snake warriors. Holding the net, of course, was the Samurai in his mechanical robot suit.

The maidens changed their cheer. "Go, Samurai, go!"

"Ninjaaago!" Kai cried, using Spinjitzu to become a **swirling tornado**. He whirled toward the Samurai—who shot out another net and stopped Kai in his tracks.

"Hey, what's going on?" Kai asked.

When Cole found out about a Serpentine attack in the Caves of Despair, he rushed to

the scene. Inside the large, dark cavern, the Samurai was already battling a small army of Fangpyres and Venomari. Cole stealthily moved from rock to rock, trying to sneak up on the Samurai.

"Now I've got you," he whispered. Then he jumped onto the Samurai's giant robot arm.

Whoosh! The Samurai pressed a button and the arm broke apart, launching Cole clear across the cave.

Jay had his own idea about how to capture the Samurai. He decided to set a trap. He put on a blonde wig and a pink dress and lay down on some railroad tracks. He could hear a train huffing and puffing in the distance. He knew the Samurai would have to rescue him—and then Jay could surprise him.

"Help! Samurai!" Jay called out in a high-pitched voice.

The Samurai flew down from the sky and studied Jay for a minute. Then he used

his powerful robot hands to tear apart the train tracks next to Jay and put them back together like a puzzle. He re-routed the train, which sailed safely past Jay. The Samurai had seen through his disguise.

"Stupid Samurai!" Jay yelled.

While the ninja were trying to capture the Samurai, they had to take turns babysitting Lloyd. None of them liked it. When it was Kai's turn, he took Lloyd to Ninjago City and dropped him off at the Kiddie Arcade.

"Just play a few games and stay put while I look around," Kai told him. "I have a feeling the Samurai may show up."

"Let me help," Lloyd begged.

"No," Kai said firmly.

"Come on," Lloyd whined. He glanced up at the arcade window, which was filled with oversized stuffed animals and silly toys. "At least drop me off at a decent arcade."

"Sorry, Shorty," Kai said. Then he sped off

in his Blade Cycle, leaving Lloyd in a cloud of dust.

Lloyd turned to go into the arcade — but then he heard a familiar-sounding voice.

"I hear he found it. And everyone is gathering again."

That voice was definitely Serpentine, Lloyd knew. He walked to the edge of the building and peered down the long, dark alleyway.

He was right. A group of Serpentine from different tribes was gathered in the shadows.

"Impossible," said a Fangpyre soldier. "The Lost City does not exist."

"Well, it isn't lost anymore," said the first speaker, a Hypnobrai. Then he laughed. "And I hear **there's going to be a fight**."

"A fight? Count me in!"

The Serpentine walked away from the alley, and Lloyd cautiously followed them, making sure he wasn't seen. He watched them line up to get on a big green bus.

"All aboard!" cried the Hypnobrai. "Next stop: Ouroboros!"

Could the bus really be going to the Lost City of legend? Lloyd wondered. He had heard the Serpentine discuss the city before. Cole and Sensei Wu had warned that it would be dangerous for all of the tribes to unite. Maybe that's what they were planning to do in Ouroboros. If so, this was a big discovery. He should go tell Sensei Wu . . . or . . .

I'll handle this myself, Lloyd thought. *Then I'll prove that I can be a ninja, too!*

Thinking quickly, Lloyd hurried back to the street. He remembered the toys and stuffed animals he had seen in the arcade window. He ducked inside and came out wearing a big snake head and carrying two maracas. When he shook them, they made a rattling sound. Then he topped off the outfit with a pair of red glasses and some fake fangs. He looked like one of the

two-legged Serpentine warriors.

Lloyd raced back to the bus just as it was about to take off. He climbed up the steps.

"Hey, you, hold it there," said the Hypnobrai from the alley.

Lloyd gulped. Had the Serpentine seen through his disguise?

"Last one in closes the door," the Hypnobrai hissed.

"*Sssure* thing," Lloyd said, relieved.

He climbed aboard and tried to blend in. The bus left Ninjago City and headed across barren desert. It seemed to take forever.

Finally, just as the moon was rising, Lloyd looked out the window and spotted a tall, stone statue of a Serpentine. He gasped as he saw a city sprawl out before him, made up of hundreds of buildings. Statues of Serpentine lined every road.

"The Lost City of Ouroboros is real!" Lloyd whispered.

CHAPTER 3

The bus stopped in front of a huge circular coliseum with spectator seats cut out of the sandstone. Lloyd followed the other Serpentine as they filed into the arena, which was already filled with hundreds of snake warriors. All of them were cheering and shouting. They were definitely **ready for a fight**.

Across the coliseum from Lloyd, an enormous statue of a serpent towered above the stands. The statue was flanked by two tall pillars, and one was dripping with evil-looking green venom.

Is that the Great Devourer? Lloyd wondered. He shuddered. It was scary to imagine what would happen if that thing came to life.

Underneath the statue, Pythor surveyed the scene in front of him. Next to him was Scales, the Hypnobrai general.

"Just do as I've said, and I promise you will be my second-in-command . . . forever," Pythor promised Scales.

Scales bowed respectfully, and then the two Serpentine stuffed cotton balls in their ears. Pythor slithered forward and addressed the unruly crowd.

"I bring you together, to the Lost City of Ouroboros, before the statue of our very own Great Devourer, to speak of unity!" Pythor shouted.

But the snake warriors weren't interested in speeches.

"Where are the fights?" yelled one.

"When's the big show?" hissed another.

Then the Serpentine began to chant, "Slither Pit! Slither Pit! Slither Pit!"

With an angry roar, Pythor leaped into the circle-shaped Slither Pit in the center of the coliseum.

"You want a show?" he asked. "You want to see a fight? I ask for your allegiance but you will not give it . . . so I will take it!"

He crawled along the pit, headed toward the Serpentine generals, who were lined up on the other side. Each general held a golden staff with a serpent's head — the key to each tribe's power.

"What are you saying?" asked the two-headed Fangpyre general.

"I challenge the four tribe generals for their staffs *and* their allegiance!" Pythor cried. "At once!"

The Serpentine in the stands erupted. This was what they'd been waiting for!

The four generals began to slither toward Pythor.

"I fought hard for this staff, and will not give it up easily!" hissed the green Venomari general.

The Constrictai general's orange scales gleamed in the moonlight. "There's no way he can defeat the four of us at once," he said confidently. Then he tried to strike Pythor with his staff, but Pythor spun around and lashed at him with his long, purple tail.

The Venomari general attacked next, swinging his staff.

Bam! Pythor clocked him with a hard punch.

Then the Fangpyre general lashed out, but Pythor whipped him with his tail.

Angry, the four generals all lunged at Pythor at once. He fell to the ground. From the stands, it looked like Pythor was at the mercy of the generals.

But Scales was only pretending to fight. He slipped him the Sacred Flute, and Pythor began to play. He and Scales couldn't hear

it because of the cotton in their ears.

Lloyd realized what was happening. "He's using the Sacred Flute against his own," he whispered to himself.

The generals held their ears and cried out in pain. Scales did, too, but he was pretending again. He threw down his staff and pretended to faint.

Bam! Pow! Smack! Pythor quickly took down the remaining three generals. Each one dropped his staff.

"Bow to your master!" he commanded them.

The four generals all bowed.

Then Pythor addressed the crowd. "Bow to your master, Serpentine!" he cried in a **booming** voice.

To the snake warriors, it looked like Pythor had won fair and square. They all bowed respectfully. Lloyd bowed, too, but when he lowered his head, his fake snake head started to slide off. When he reached up to

grab it, he dropped his maracas. They fell with a clatter into the Slither Pit.

Pythor heard the noise and spun around quickly, spying the maracas. His magenta eyes glowed with suspicion. As he looked up into the stands, Lloyd broke into a run. But the Hypnobrai next to him grabbed him by the arm and pulled him back. Lloyd's snake head, glasses, and fangs all fell off.

The Serpentine standing next to him grabbed him before he had a chance to run. "Where do you think you're going?" he demanded.

Pythor looked up in the stands, recognizing him immediately.

"Lloyd?"

CHAPTER 4

Back on *Destiny's Bounty,* the ninja sat around the tea table with Nya, complaining about the Samurai.

"Trying to find out the Samurai's identity is more of a nuisance than the snakes," Cole said.

"The guy's elusive. He's like a ghost. One moment he's there, the next he's gone!" Jay added.

"I'm starting to believe we might never catch him," Zane admitted.

"I think it's safe to say, none of us are

closer to proving we're the Green Ninja," Kai said sadly.

Sensei Wu walked in, smiling. It was nice to see his ninja working hard at something.

"Looks like iron sharpening iron," he said. "You're getting closer to your true potential."

Then he looked around the table. "Where is my nephew? I thought you were looking after him."

"I thought Cole was going to pick him up," Kai said.

"I went to the arcade, but he wasn't there," Cole explained. "Jay was —"

"Don't bring me into this, I babysat yesterday," Jay said defensively.

Zane was concerned. "Sensei, we have not seen him."

A worried look crossed Sensei Wu's face. "We must find the boy."

The ninja hurried back to Ninjago City and headed to the arcade.

"Lloyd?" Kai called out as he opened the door, but Lloyd was nowhere in sight.

"He was right here," Kai said, pointing to the door where he had left Lloyd. "Someone must have seen him."

Then Cole noticed something—a security camera mounted on a light post outside the door. He took the tape from the camera and they quickly returned to the ship to analyze it. It wasn't long before they spotted Lloyd on the tape—wearing a snake costume and heading into the alley.

"There's the pipsqueak!" Kai said.

"What is he up to?" Jay wondered aloud.

The ninja returned to the alleyway. Zane spotted child-sized footprints and followed them.

"I sense these are Lloyd's footprints, but they come to an end here," he said. "Why?"

Kai pointed to the tire tracks left by the bus. "Something tells me we're going for a ride. Come on, guys!"

They transformed their Weapons into vehicles, and they followed the tracks across the desert. Their **super-charged** rides were a lot faster than the bus, but the journey still took a long time. They skidded to a stop when they came to the stone Serpentine statues.

"What *is* this place?" Cole asked.

"Looks like Snake City," Jay guessed.

"Let's get a closer look," Kai suggested.

Serpentine warriors guarded the city entrance, so the ninja transformed their vehicles back into Weapons and took to the rooftops. They cautiously made their way toward the coliseum, jumping from building to building.

When they reached the arena, they jumped down and hid behind a large stone pillar. The sight of hundreds of Serpentine gathered together was truly amazing.

"It appears Pythor has successfully united the tribes," Zane remarked.

"Why didn't we get an invitation? My feelings are hurt," Jay joked.

"There's Lloyd!" Kai cried, pointing.

Poor Lloyd was trapped in a black metal cage hanging from the statue of the Great Devourer.

"And look at who they worship," Jay said, pointing to the evil-looking giant statue.

"Let me guess. The Great Devourer," Cole said grimly.

"All the more reason to get Lloyd out of here," Kai said with determination. He drew the Sword of Fire. "This comes to an end today!"

Cole, Zane, and Jay all unleashed their weapons. They charged into the arena as a team.

Clank! A metal cage dropped from above, trapping them. Their Weapons flew out of their hands and landed just out of reach.

Pythor slithered up to them with a pleased look on his face.

"Looks like we've caught the main event," he said, licking his lips.

The ninja were helpless to fight back as a group of sword-wielding snake warriors surrounded them. The cage rose up, and the soldiers marched them into the Slither Pit.

"'Main event'? What do you think he meant by 'main event'?" Jay asked.

"I have a feeling *we're* the main event," Kai told him.

Cole looked around at the hundreds of cheering Serpentine. "Or the main course," he quipped.

"Don't worry," Kai said in a panicked voice. "The Samurai could still come around to save us."

Then Pythor made an announcement from his perch underneath the statue of the Great Devourer.

"You say you want a battle, and I give you one!" he cried. "I give you ninja versus . . . samurai!"

CHAPTER 5

The ninja gasped as a gate opened up in the wall across from them. The Samurai marched out, wearing his metal exo-suit. Heavy chains around his robot wrists kept him tied to the gate. Two Serpentine warriors released the chains, and the Samurai stomped forward.

"What?" Jay asked angrily. "We have to fight the Samurai? But we don't even have our Golden Weapons, and he has that hulking thing of armor. It's not fair!"

Pythor had no interest in a fair fight. "I want to see once and for all who is the greatest

hero!" he announced. "Is it samurai or ninja? Only the victor will be allowed to leave."

Kai nodded to his friends. "Stay together."

"Perhaps he can join our team to fight our way out," Zane said. "After all, he hates the Serpentine, too."

The Samurai shot a spinning metal disc right at the ninja. They had to jump in different directions to dodge it.

"Scratch that," Cole said. "He is *not* on our team!"

The Samurai barreled forward and swung at the ninja with his huge robot hand. Zane, Cole, and Kai dodged out of the way, and Jay expertly flipped over the hand, avoiding the blow.

The four ninja regrouped, forming a defensive line. The Samurai sent another metal disc spinning toward them. Cole, Zane, and Kai scattered, and Jay ducked as the disc soared over his head.

"Ha-ha! Missed me!" he cried. But the

blade boomeranged back and struck the back of his helmet.

"Ow!" Jay yelled, and the Serpentine cheered. His friends ran up to him.

Then the Samurai drew a huge silver sword. He jumped high in the air and then brought the sword down on the ninja. Once again, they had to jump and flip to dodge the attack.

"Tornado of Creation?" Zane asked when they were back on their feet.

The other ninja nodded. This Spinjitzu move was nearly impossible to beat because it involved all four of their powers.

"Earth!" Cole cried, becoming a spinning whirlwind.

"Fire!" yelled Kai as he created his Spinjitzu tornado.

"Ice!" cried Zane.

"Lightning!" yelled Jay.

The four separate tornadoes sparked with energy as they spun around the Slither

Pit. Fearful of what was about to happen, the Samurai took a step backward.

"Ninjaaaaago!" the ninja yelled together.

Then the four tornadoes collided, creating one **massive whirl-wind** that glowed with white, blue, black, and red light. The powerful tornado sucked any loose object in the arena toward it—rocks, swords, even the candy that the Serpentine were eating in the stands.

When the tornado stopped spinning, the objects had been combined to create an entirely new object: a giant slingshot with a huge spiked ball nestled in the sling. The four ninja pulled back on the sling and sent the spiked ball flying across the Slither Pit.

Bam! The ball knocked into the Samurai, sending him colliding into Pythor and Scales.

The ninja raced forward to finish the fight, but Pythor pulled a serpent-shaped lever next to him. Sharp stone spikes popped up from the arena floor, blocking their path. The

ninja looked around and saw that the spikes formed a spiral all around the Slither Pit.

"Why can't anyone play fair?" Jay complained.

Pythor grinned and pulled the lever again. The floor of the arena rose and then tilted, knocking them off of their feet. Flames burst up all around the fighting area. The ninja and the Samurai slid down the slanted floor and had to grab on to the spikes to keep from sliding off into the fire. "Can this get any worse?" Cole asked.

The Samurai turned to the ninja and spoke in a low voice. "We must continue to make it appear that we are fighting for real," he said.

"We're *not* fighting for real?" Jay asked.

"Keep up the charade and hold on to my exo-suit," the Samurai instructed.

The ninja had no choice but to trust the Samurai. With a cry, they all jumped on the exo-suit, pretending to attack the Samurai. Then the Samurai pressed a button,

and two jet thrusters burst into flame on the bottom of his robot feet. As the ninja hung on, the suit began to lift off into the sky, leaving plumes of black smoke in its wake.

Then the jet thrusters began to sputter and shake.

"There's too much weight!" Kai cried.

The Samurai opened the cage on the exo-suit's chest and jumped back down into the arena. Now that the suit was lighter, it quickly zoomed away.

"I can't believe he just saved us!" Cole yelled.

"He stole our thunder again!" Kai cried angrily.

"I hate that samurai!" Jay shouted.

Then they soared away from the arena to safety.

CHAPTER 6

"Go, ninja, go!" Lloyd yelled as the ninja soared away. Pythor looked furious.

The Samurai landed on the stands.

Pow! Pow! He knocked down two snake warriors with a quick left hand followed by a quick right. Then he jumped into the Slither Pit and raced to Lloyd's cage.

Pythor was faster. He yanked open the cage door and pulled Lloyd to him.

"Get him!" he yelled to his soldiers.

At the command, snake warriors surrounded the Samurai. If he was going to escape, he had to do it now — without Lloyd.

But he didn't have to leave empty-handed. The Samurai pressed a button on his left sleeve and pointed it at the ninja's four Golden Weapons, which were propped up against the statue of the Great Devourer.

"Magnetizer activated," the Samurai said, and a blue beam shot out. It latched on to the four Weapons, and they floated to the Samurai. He jumped up, spinning, to catch the Weapons in midair. Then he stuffed them into a special pack.

But the snake warriors were coming closer. Thinking quickly, the Samurai hurled a metal disc at the Slither Pit's control button. It hit the button and the arena tilted.

"Aaaaaah!" The Serpentine cried out as they slid down toward the flames under the pit. The Samurai rocketed upward. Lloyd gazed up at him with admiration.

The Samurai waved good-bye to Pythor, who roared with anger. Then he flew off into the sky, carrying the Golden Weapons with him.

Meanwhile, the Samurai's exo-suit was rocketing out of control, spinning and swooping in the sky. The ninja hung on tightly.

"How do you turn this thing off?" Kai yelled.

But there was no off button. The suit crash-landed on the sandy floor of the desert, bouncing again and again before it finally came to a stop. The impact sent the four ninja across the yellow desert sand.

Bruised and shaken, Jay got to his feet and looked around. The crash had kicked up a lot of sand, and he shielded his eyes to get a better look. They were surrounded by sand dunes, and he could make out the battered exo-suit. Then he saw Zane in his white uniform stand up and wave. And there was Cole. But one ninja was missing.

Kai had landed facedown yards away next to a large sand dune, so his friends couldn't see him. He pulled himself out and then looked around, but all he could see was miles of sand.

Then he saw a flash of red speeding across the blue sky.

"The Samurai?" Kai wondered aloud. He watched as the Samurai's jet pack began to spit out thick, black smoke. The jet pack sputtered, and now it was the Samurai's turn to make a crash-landing.

Bam! It didn't look good. Kai raced forward to help. When he arrived, the Samurai had his back to him. His helmet looked broken, and Kai watched as the Samurai took it off to fix it.

This is my chance! Kai thought, his heart beating with excitement. *Once I see the Samurai's face, I will know his real identity. Then everyone will have to agree that I am the Green Ninja!*

Underneath the helmet was a head of shiny black hair. Kai gasped, and the Samurai spun around at the sound. He knew that face.

It was his sister, Nya!

CHAPTER 7

Nya?" Kai asked in disbelief.

Nya quickly tried to put the broken helmet back on.

"Uh, steer clear, ninja! Don't look!" she said. But the device she used to make her voice sound deeper wasn't working. With a sigh, Nya took off the helmet once more.

"I don't understand," Kai said. "*You're* the Samurai?"

"It was always a boy's club," Nya explained. "You never let me try to help. So I found my own way to be a hero. Are you mad?"

"Mad? Of course not," her brother replied.

"It's just . . . all this time, I've been trying to protect *you*, and you never needed it. You're amazing!"

Nya grinned and playfully punched her brother in the shoulder.

"Girl power!" she cheered. Then her smile was replaced by a worried look. "You're not gonna tell the others, are you?"

"But we have a bet," Kai said. "We said whoever caught the Samurai would be the Green . . ."

Kai didn't have the heart to finish his sentence when he saw the look on Nya's face. She looked horrified at the idea that the others would find out her secret.

"Of course I won't say anything," Kai said with a sigh. Being the Green Ninja meant a lot to him — but his sister meant even more.

He pointed to Nya's jet pack. "So how did you make all this stuff?"

"You'd be surprised to know how much spare time I had waiting for you guys to come

back from your missions," Nya told him.

She handed him the red pack containing **the Golden Weapons**. "You'd better head back before anyone gets suspicious," she told him. "We'll have to rescue Lloyd another day."

Kai nodded. A serious look crossed his face. "Nya, whenever I get in trouble, the other three always have my back," he said. "But you . . . just . . . be careful, okay?"

Nya nodded. "Promise."

"But how are you going to get back?" Kai asked her.

Nya grinned. "I have my ways!" she replied, picking up her helmet and pressing a button.

On the other side of the desert, Jay, Cole, and Zane were searching for Kai when they heard the exo-suit begin to beep in the distance. Then they heard the engines begin to fire up.

"Quick! Get it! It's going to get away!" Jay yelled.

They ran as fast as they could, but it was no use. The exo-suit flew away without them, trailing plumes of black smoke in its wake. They stopped and doubled over, trying to catch their breath.

"Great," Jay complained. "Now we lost Kai, the Samurai suit is gone, *and* we have no way to get home."

Cole turned and looked at the top of the dune behind them.

"I wouldn't say that," he remarked.

Zane and Jay turned to see Kai making his way over the hill—carrying the four Golden Weapons!

"It's about time! Now let's get out of this sand pit!" Jay said.

CHAPTER 8

Using the Golden Weapons, the ninja made it back to *Destiny's Bounty*. Nya was already there, thanks to the exo-suit. But no one—except for Kai, of course—knew that she had even been gone.

The ship soared above the clouds. White stars twinkled in the deep blue sky, casting a blue glow over the whole ship. As the ninja got ready for bed, they talked about the day's events with Sensei Wu.

"He was all mysterious," Kai said as he brushed his teeth. "Never said a word. Just handed me the Golden Weapons then